Vet

ILLUSTRATED BY JESS STOCKHAM

These tablets will make your dog feel better.

You'll need to bring him back next week.

How long before the vet will see us?

All that barking will frighten the other animals!

I'll push the needle in just under the skin.

I'll hold her still. Will it hurt her?

I had an injection when I was small.

It will protect him from all kinds of illness.

Let's brush her carefully to see if she has any fleas.

Special drops on her neck will make them go away.

His tummy is swollen. He may have worms.

We can give him a tablet that will clear them up.

When I pick her up, her claws scratch me. Ouch!

I'll cut her nails short. It won't hurt her at all.

He can't eat. His teeth are too long. We'll trim them.

I'm glad my teeth don't keep on growing like that!

He cut his paw when we were at the park.

Now we've cleaned it, we'll bandage it up.

He's hurt his wing. I think he flew into something.

I'll tape it up. We'll keep him here until he's better.

My corn snake is ill. I think he has mites.

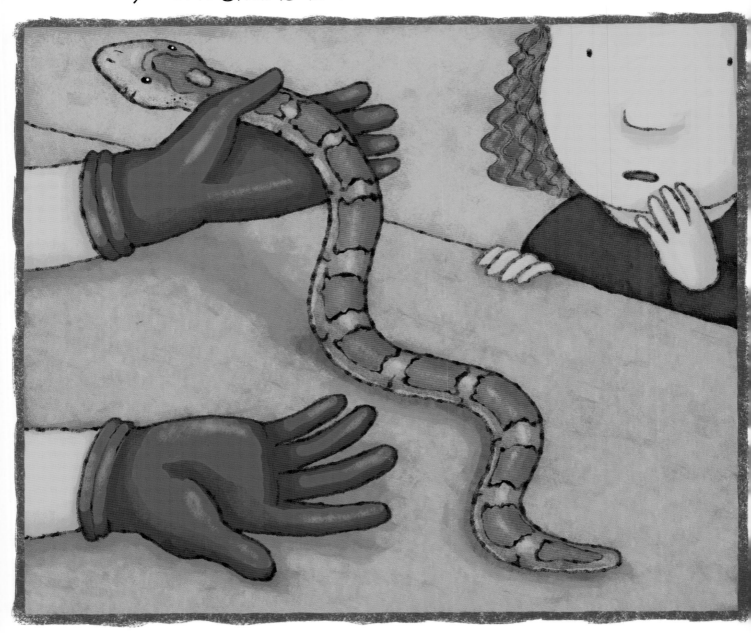

He'll feel better if we give him a bath.

Is my tortoise healthy enough to hibernate?

Let's check him over. We'll measure and weigh him.

She isn't eating much or running about. Is she ok?

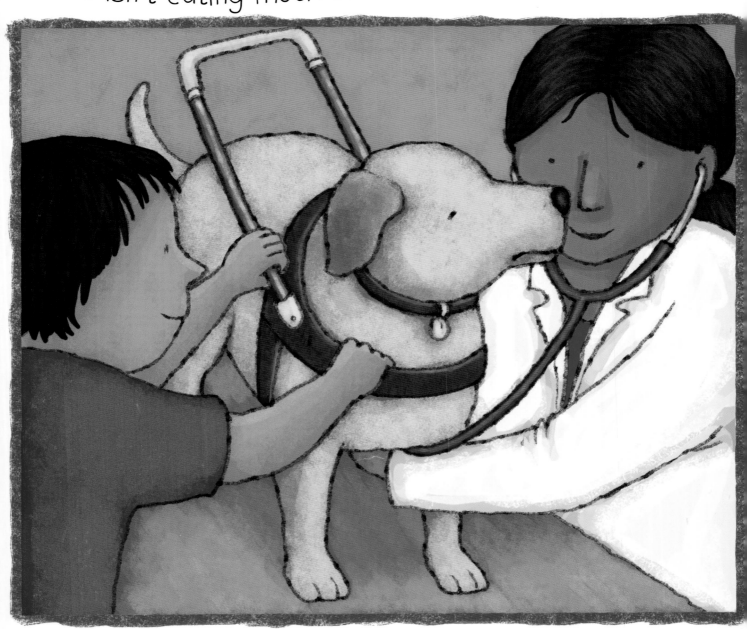

I'll listen to her heartbeat with my stethoscope.

I'll check her temperature with my thermometer.

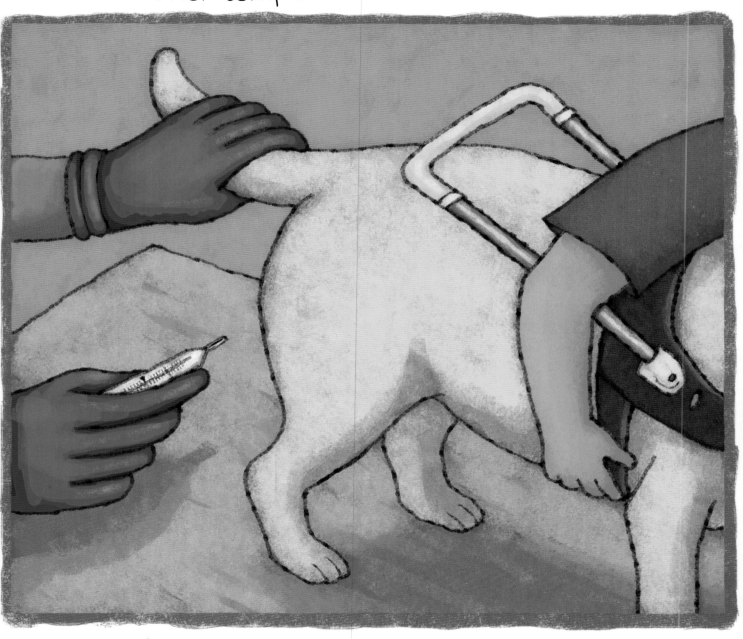

She should feel better after taking some medicine.

With this, I can see whether her eyes are clear.

Has she been eating and drinking normally?

Leave her here overnight. We'll look after her.

Will I be able to pick her up tomorrow?

Your paw won't get better if you chew your bandage.

You won't be able to chew it with that collar on!

You do look funny! You don't like it, do you?

We'll remove it when your paw has healed.

He's very big. Make sure he doesn't fall off the scales!

He's been eating too much. He needs to eat less.

He has lots of teeth, but he doesn't bite me.

Cleaning them like this keeps them healthy.

She's quite unwell. She has a lump on her side.

I'm afraid she might not live much longer.

Your cat is pregnant. She's going to have kittens.

Hooray! How many? Will they look like her?

She's fine now! You can take her home.

Can you hear her purr? She must be happy to see me!